George Dalziel, Edward Dalziel

The child's coloured gift book : with one hundred illustrations

George Dalziel, Edward Dalziel

The child's coloured gift book : with one hundred illustrations

ISBN/EAN: 9783337214661

Printed in Europe, USA, Canada, Australia, Japan

Cover: Foto ©Andreas Hilbeck / pixelio.de

More available books at **www.hansebooks.com**

FRONTISPIECE.

THE CHILD'S

COLOURED GIFT BOOK.

***

With One Hundred Illustrations.

LONDON:

GEORGE ROUTLEDGE AND SONS,

THE BROADWAY, LUDGATE.

NEW YORK: 416, BROOME STREET.

1867.

THE

FARM YARD

ALPHABET.

A stands for the Ass, who eats thistles and grass;
He is useful and patient, though only an Ass.

B for the Bees, that fly out here and there,
And bring to the hives the sweet honey with care.

C for the Cows, in the shade of the
   trees ;
They are chewing the cud, and seem
   quite at their ease.

D for Ducks, swimming, diving, and
    playing together;
They care not for rain nor the stormiest
    weather.

E for the Eggs, which we find in
    the nest;
They still feel quite warm, from the
    hen's downy breast.

F are the Fowls: the hens and the cocks.

Take care, my fine birdies, beware of the fox.

G is the Goat, with two kids young
   and gay;
They run to their mother, then scamper
   away.

H is the Horse, so sleek and so
strong ;
He draws the hay-cart to the meadow
along.

I is the Isle; and I'll mention my wish
To sit on the bank, in the summer, and fish.

K are the Kittens, that live in the
stable;
They will catch all the mice as soon
as they're able.

L is for Lucy, who waits at the
    stile,
And puts down the pail, for she's resting
    awhile.

M is the Milk, which is good,
      Pussy thinks,
And so, uninvited and slyly, she
      drinks.

N stands for the Nuts; and when lessons are done,
Two boys can go nutting much better than one.

O for the Owl, that flies out in the night,
And sails o'er the barn in the quiet moonlight.

P for some Pigs, which have strayed
from their sty,
But of course will return there to bed
by-and-by.

Q stands for the Quince I have
plucked from a tree,
To flavour the tart Mary's making for
me.

R for the Rabbits, white, spotted, and gray ;
Just see how that little one nibbles away.

S for the Sheep, with their coats of
    soft wool.
They stand in the meadows so pleasant
    and cool.

T for the Turkey, who stately doth
    sail,
With long sweeping wings and wide-
    spreading tail.

V for the Vine, growing high on the
    wall;
Take care, little boy, or you surely will
    fall.

W for Waggon, that stands empty alone
Near the trees in the fields when the horses are gone.

X, put on a barrel, is intended to tell
The strength of the beer, and its flavour
as well.

Y is the Yard, where the chicks love
    to feed
On the oats, and the barley, and other
    good seed.

Z is for Zachary, shutting the gate;
So Good Night, little children; it's
getting quite late.

TOM THUMB'S

ALPHABET.

A was an Archer,
who shot at a frog.

B was a Butcher,
who had a great dog.

C was a Captain,
all covered with lace.

D was a Drummer,
who played with a grace.

E was an Esquire,
with pride on his brow.

F was a Farmer,
who followed the plough.

G was a Gamester,
who had but ill-luck.

H was a Hunter,
who hunted a buck.

I was an Italian,
  who had a white mouse,
Whom John the footman
  drove from the house.

K was a King,
so mighty and grand.

L was a Lady,
who had a white hand.

M was a Miser,
who hoarded up gold.

N was a Nobleman, gallant and bold.

O was an Organ-Boy,
who played for his bread.

P a Policeman,
of bad boys the dread.

Q was a Quaker,
who would not bow down.

R was a Robber,
who prowled about town.

S was a Sailor,
who spent all he got.

T was a Tinker,
who mended a pot.

V was a Veteran,
who never knew fear.

W was a Waiter,
with dinners in store.

X was Expensive,
and so became poor.

Y was a Youth,
who did not like school.

Z was a Zany,
who looked a great fool.

LEIGHTON, BR⁰S.

THE CHILD'S

BOOK OF TRADES.

THE ARTIST.

HERE is an Artist painting a picture.
It is the portrait of a lady. The
picture is being painted upon canvass,
with brushes of different sizes made
from the hair of animals, and the stand
upon which the picture rests is called
an easel. The Artist stands near the
easel, and the lady is seated at a
little distance from him. Her chair
is placed on a dais so that the Artist
may have a full view of her.

I hope ma'am you take care to sit still; for if you do not, the Artist cannot make your picture like, and he looks as if he was trying very much.

I do not think it is like yet, but it looks more good-natured and smiling than you do. You look rather cross, which is a pity.

What a fine dress you have put on! The feathers are very grand, and you have got a sort of golden crown besides. The artist has not done it well at all. He has not put points enough, and the feathers look too round and thick, but they are not done yet, and he will make the crown right, I dare say. What large red bows you have put on your blue dress! It is very fine indeed.

The artist has put you all out to one side in the picture. I wonder what he is going to paint in that empty part. Perhaps there is going to be another grand lady sitting by you.

What bright colours the artist has got on his palette! That flat wooden

thing he holds in his hand is called a
palette, and that is his brush in his
other hand   He is going to dip his
brush in the red paint.   I suppose he
is going to do the bows, or perhaps the
red chair.

I think sir, that if that lion was alive you would not go so near him, nor peep into his cage as you are doing. It is only a stuffed lion in a glass case. Take care you do not break the glass with your umbrella.

I wonder where the lion came from, and where he lived when he was alive! He is a very large lion! What a great head he has! I think he must have come from Africa.

We cannot see what is in the case behind the gentleman. We can just see a little face of some creature in that case at the end where a lady and gentleman are standing. I think it must be a monkey. But it must be stuffed too. A monkey could not live in a glass case for want of air; and if it was in a cage you could not venture so near it as the lady is, unless it was of some very gentle, quiet kind. Monkeys are so full of tricks and mischief. One day a lady was standing near a cage full of them, laughing at their funny ways, and never saw that one of them was slowly creeping and creeping near her, till in a moment it darted out its little black hand, seized her parasol and climbed up to the top of the cage with it and broke it to pieces.

Were you ever in a Blacksmith's Forge? At the entrance into most villages, the Blacksmith is to be seen As you pass you hear his heavy hammer banging away, and the fire roaring as another man or boy in the corner blows the bellows. If you look in, you see the blacksmith hammering at a piece of red-hot iron, and the sparks fly out at every stroke. He has that hot fire to make the iron red-hot, and do you know why he wants his iron to be red-hot? It is because then it is soft, and he can hammer it into any shape he likes. When iron is cold it is quite hard.

Another day you may see the blacksmith shoeing a horse. The blacksmith makes horse shoes of iron, and as each of his customers wants two pair, he has a great many to make. You may see horse shoes hanging on the wall behind him, ready for his customers when they come. Some are large, for cart horses; some middle-sized for riding horses; some little for ponies. He nails them

on the horse's hoof. It does not hurt,
because the hoof is hard and has no
feeling. But wild horses wear no shoes,
and some people think they are better
without them, at least, unless they have
hard work on stones or pavement.

This workman is called an Engineer. His trade is to make all manner of great engines and machines that are made of brass and iron. You have, I dare say, sometimes gone by a railway train, and have seen the engine that goes hissing and puffing along, pulling all the carriages after it. These engines are made by engineers. You may see in the picture, some of the wheels lying on the floor, and a tube or great pipe that is to be some part of an engine, and brass chains, and bolts and other things.

Perhaps, some day, you may go to see a factory where they spin cotton or flax, or weave calico or muslin. These things are done by machines that can do the work of a hundred men a hundred times faster than the men could. All these machines are made by engineers.

In England, there is so much iron and so much coal, that a great many machines are made besides those used in England itself, and sent to other

countries. Do you know what the coal
is for? The iron could not be got out
of the stone it is found in without great
heat; and then it is so hard, that till it
is made red-hot in the fire it cannot be
made into anything useful.

I think that, of all trades, I should like best to be a Gardener. How nice it is to work among pretty flowers; and to see the things that you have planted growing up from little weak plants, and throwing out leaves and buds and bright flowers. This gardener, in the picture, seems to have reared a great many scarlet geraniums. I think he is going to turn one out of the pot and put it in the ground. The little tool he holds in his hand is called a trowel. He will dig a hole in the ground with it; then he will get the plant out of the pot and put it in. There it will grow to be very large and throw out plenty of flowers, now it has room for its roots. But then, the worst of it is, that it cannot bear the winter, so he must take it up before the frost comes, and in doing that, he may kill it. The best way is to cut off some of its branches early in autumn, and plant them in pots. If properly trimmed and cut, all the branches, or slips, as

people call them, will take root and
grow into plants, and he will keep them
in warm frames or houses through the
winter, and in spring they will be nice
and bushy, and if he has saved the old
root too, so much the better.

Harvest time is come, and the corn
is ripe. In the picture you see a field
of wheat, gold colour, and ready for
the reaper, and the reaper is there with
his sickle beginning to cut it down.
You may know wheat from other kinds

of corn by its standing upright. Barley droops its head and has long spines growing by the grains that people call its beard. Oats grow light and feathery, like some of the wild grasses.

Bread is made of wheat. The farmer sows it in his fields, and it springs up and ripens. Then the reaper cuts it down. By and bye, it is thrashed, that is, beaten to get the grains of wheat away from the stalks, which are called straw, and are very useful too. Bonnets, hats, baskets, mats, and many other things are made of straw, and cattle and horses want it to lie upon for beds. When the grains are out of the straw they are sent to the miller to grind in his mill. You have seen a windmill, I dare say, and perhaps you have seen a water-mill, with a great wheel turned by running water instead of sails turned by the wind; and when the miller has ground the wheat into flour, the baker buys it and makes the bread.

If you have ever been at the sea-
side, you must have seen the shrimps
that people buy for breakfast, or if you
live in London you must have seen the
little shrimps in the shops. This man
is catching them. Shrimps are little

creatures that live in the sand, and the time to catch them is when the tide flows over the sand, and the water is not deeper than to cover the man's feet, for then they jump about in the water, and as he pushes his net on before him, numbers jump into it, and he takes his net out every now and then, puts the shrimps into his basket, and goes on again to catch more. The poor little shrimps soon die when they are out of the water. When the shrimper has caught enough, he takes them to the fishmonger and sells them to him, and goes home and gives the money to his wife to buy food. The fishmonger boils the shrimps and sells them to whoever will buy. Shrimps have no colour till they are boiled.

Many boys are shrimpers, and earn a good deal by it to help their fathers and mothers. The work is not too hard for them.

Do you see in the picture the boats in the sea, and the sea-birds flying?

There was a poor widow who had a little boy. He never could learn to read. So she sent him to the farmer's, but he was turned off. When he grew to be a young lad he never got wages like the others. His name was

Roger, but every one called him Hodge. One summer, the poor widow fell sick and there was no food in the house. Hodge sat by her and cried. "Don't cry, dear!" she said, "We must be patient." "Oh, mother!" sobbed Hodge, "You want your cup of tea, and there's none for you."

Hodge got up at daybreak and went out. He stood about till the farmer came out on his strong horse. Then he went up to the farmer. You may see him in the picture. "Please sir, I want work in the hay," said Hodge. "Well, my man, I want hands," said the farmer, "go and begin!" So Hodge worked like a lion. Whenever he felt lazy, he thought to himself "mother's cup of tea." At night he got half-a-crown like the rest. He went to the shop, bought tea, sugar, milk, bread and butter; went home, boiled the kettle, and helped his mother. She never liked her tea so much before. She was so happy that she got well, and Hodge was less lazy always after.

What a strong boot the Cobbler is mending! I think he will make it as good as new. He seems to have plenty of work. I have seen some cobblers with ten or more pairs of shoes and boots lying round them not touched, and the people kept coming, and saying, "Are my boots done yet?" "When shall I have my shoes?" This cobbler looks as if he was a good worker.

Do you know that it was a poor cobbler that first began a ragged school? His name was John Pounds. As he sat at work, he felt very sorry to see a number of poor ragged children, boys and girls, idling about in the street; sometimes fighting, sometimes doing mischief; so he thought he would try to do something for them. He called some of them in, and began to talk to them, and teach them what he knew, and that they should love one another and not fight, and that they should try to find some work to do instead of

being idle. More and more came into
his little shop, and he got easy books
and taught them to read, and taught
them to say little hymns. Now there
are many ragged schools, but John
Pounds began them.

These poor Dressmakers have been at work since eight o'clock in the morning, and now they are working by candle-light, late at night. The clock tells the hour. It is nearly ten minutes past twelve. How pale and tired they look!

I am sure that if the fine ladies who are going to wear those dresses knew how much the poor girls had to suffer, while they worked at them, they would be very sorry. Perhaps that light dress, all trimmed with pink ribbons and roses, is for a young lady about the same age as the young girl who is making it. Perhaps she will wear it at a ball, and dance gaily, and look pretty in it. She little thinks what weary fingers fixed on those bright ribbons and roses. There are many kind ladies who do think of it, and who are trying to prevent it. They tell other ladies that they ought not to order dresses in a hurry, nor say "I must have my dress to-morrow." If they do, the dressmakers will have to

sit up all night to finish the work.
And these kind ladies try to make the
mistresses of the young girls think
more of these poor workers, and air the
rooms they sit in, and employ more, so
as to prevent any working so long.

This man is a Hatter. Do you know what hats are made of? When you hear the people calling out "hare skins! rabbit skins!" and see the cooks come out to sell them, you have heard one of the things hats are made of. Rabbit skins help very much in making hats.

Rabbit skins are of use for many other things, but they are very much used for hats. The hair is felted as it is called, that is, made into a close soft stuff like cloth, and made into the shape the hatter wants. Then it is a felt hat as it is called, and many hats are worn so. All those soft hats that people call wide-awakes are made of the felt, without any more being done to them. There is one lying on a chair with a bright red lining in it. But if the hatter wants to make a bright, stiff hat, such as gentlemen wear, he puts silk outside it that is made fit for his purpose. They used to put the hair of the beaver, but it is little used now. He is at work on a hat now, putting on

the silk. Those two that look white,
and are near him, he has done, and has
put silver paper over them for fear they
should be spoiled. All about the table
you see his tools, and on the floor
many boxes to put the hats in.

"Knives to grind! Scissors to grind!" We have all heard this cry in the streets. Here you may see a Knife-grinder at work. The sort of little cart or barrow he uses is made so as to turn a grindstone when he works a wheel with his foot. It is the grind-stone that sharpens the knives and scissors. If you look, you will see how he holds the knife so as to make the stone grind it. He must do it with care, or else he will grind away the steel too much. If he is a good workman he will only sharpen the edge and not wear away more than he can help. If you are near him, you will hear the stone go hissing against the steel knife, and will see sparks fly out. The stone and the steel coming to-gether so fast, strike out sparks. In the same way you may see a horse, when it gallops along a stony road, strike out sparks as his iron shoes dash among the stones.

The knife-grinder smokes a pipe as

he works. In winter, it is rather cold
work for him, so I suppose he finds his
pipe a comfort, though I should not
myself. I think the smell is anything
but nice. But the knife-grinder likes
it, and it is his affair, and not mine.

"'There is the Postman's knock! I
wonder whether he has brought the
letter!" It was little Amy that said this.
She had heard that some day a letter
was coming from grandmamma, that
was to ask her to go to see her, so Amy

hoped every day the letter would come. She looked out at the window. Yes, there was the postman. Then Amy went out of the school-room and stood on the stairs to see where the letter was taken to. Susan went to the drawing-room with it.

In a little while the door opened, and mamma came in. There was an open letter in her hand. "O mamma! is it from grandmamma?" cried Amy, start-ing up. "It is from grandmamma?" and she wants my little Amy to go to-morrow to stay for a week!" "O mamma, I am so glad," cries Amy, "only I wish you were going too." "I am going too," said mamma. Amy jumped up into mamma's arms with one bound, and clung round her neck.

Now there was no more thought of lessons that day. The boxes had to be packed, and she had to go and see her little cousins, and say good bye, and many things to do. Next morning they set out and were so happy.

Did you ever think where all the stones come from that are used for building bridges and churches, and paving streets, in England? and in Scotland, for building houses? for in Scotland they hardly ever use bricks for houses; nothing but stone. All this stone is found in the earth, and has to be got out; and the places where there is plenty of good stone to be found, and where people have worked to get it, and go on getting it out are called quarries.

Now you must think it is not very easy to bring the hard stone out of the earth. Men work at it with pickaxes, but it would take a long time to get much in that way, so they begin with blowing it up with gunpowder. They bore a hole in the stone or rock. Into the hole they pour some gunpowder. Then they get what is called a slow match, that will go on slowly burning. This they put into the hole and light the end. Then they get out of the way to a safe distance, and by and bye the gunpowder takes fire and blows up many pieces of rock with a great noise. In the picture you may see a lighted match, and men hiding down at the bottom of the quarry.

There was a poor old man who lived with his wife in a village. They had worked hard all their lives, but they had such small wages that they could not save any money, and now they were old and could not work, nor pay their rent. None of their children could help them. Their eldest son went many years ago to a far country. The next went for a soldier and was killed. The third died of a fever. Their daughters were all poor. They could not bear to go to the workhouse. It is very hard to work all your life, and at last to go there, where the old man would be put among the men, and the old woman among the women. They had lived together for forty years. It would be very dreadful for them.

So the old man thought he would try to earn some money as a tinker. He knew how to mend pots and kettles. They sold what few things they had, and he bought an iron pot for his fire, and some tools, and they went away together, and in every town and village he lighted his fire, and people gave him their old things to mend. I hope he will get work, and that he and his poor old wife may be able to live and not go to the workhouse.

These two ladies have come to see the old church. It is a fine old church, and has painted windows and old tombs, and the man is telling them whose tomb that is. Some Knight that died a great many years ago.

Then they went on to other parts of the church, and they went out into the churchyard, where there were many tombstones, and walked about among them. There they saw an old woman shading her eyes from the sun, and calling " Lizzie, Lizzie!" She said that her little grandchild had gone out with the kitten and her doll, and could not be found anywhere. The ladies helped her to look, but it was of no use. At last they went back into the church to rest, and while they were there, they heard a little voice say, " Sit still, pussy." They looked round. " Hold up your head, dolly!" said the voice again. They looked down into one of the pews and there they saw a little girl sitting on the floor with a kitten and a doll on a stool in front of her. " Ah, little Lizzie! Granny wants you," they said. So Lizzie let one of them carry her, and the other carry pussy and dolly, and they went out and soon found Granny.

LEIGHTON BROS.

LITTLE STORIES

FOR

GOOD CHILDREN.

LUCY AND HER DOLL.

HERE are some nice short tales for you, easy to read. They are called "Little Stories for Good Children." They are all about little boys and girls, and their friends, and their playthings. There is a story about a little boy who was a sailor and went to sea; and one about a little girl who went to a party; and another about a bad boy who was idle at school; and many more. We will begin with the Story of Lucy and her Doll.

There were two little girls, Lucy and Fanny. Lucy was the eldest; she was ten; Fanny was eight. Lucy went to school, but Fanny stayed at home. When she was ten, she was to go to school too.

The holidays were near. How Fanny longed for Lucy to come. Four weeks before, she began counting the days that had to pass. Then she began to think that she should like to give Lucy something. What could she give her? Suppose she gave her the doll that was bought with the money Aunt Jane sent at Christmas. She ran to the drawer to look at it. There lay the doll wrapped in silver paper. It had long, curling, golden hair and black eyes; pretty hands, and arms and feet, but no clothes. Fanny went to her mamma, and asked her if she had a piece of silk to make it a frock; so her mamma found a pretty piece of green silk, and some crimson ribbons for bows. But, besides a frock, her

mamma said she must make under-
clothes, and she gave her white calico
for them, and a pretty little pair of
shoes. There you can see Fanny, when
she had dressed the doll, giving it a
walk up and down the room.

What a pity this boy has found the bird's nest; poor little birds! They would have lived to be so happy. They would have learned of their parents how to fly through the air among the green leaves, and sing and enjoy their lives. Now they will all be dead in a very little while. A cruel boy can take away life in a moment, but all the men in the world cannot give it again; no, not all the greatest and strongest men that ever lived. Boys do not think what they do when they give pain, and take away life.

I daresay the mother and father birds are up in the tree, looking down at their poor little ones and mourning. They made the nest with care: it is made of little twigs of wood, woven together, and lined with soft, green moss, and wool that a sheep had left on a furze-bush; and horse-hair, that a poney had dropped out of his tail as he whisked it about to drive away the flies. They built it in a forked branch

of that tree; then the hen-bird laid six pretty little blue eggs in it; then she sat on them till they were hatched; and, after that, she and her mate flew about and found food for them. Now it is all over. Poor little birds!

There was a little girl called Jessie, who had an aunt, who lived in the country, and Jessie went to stay a week with her. It was dark when the train stopped, and Jessie's aunt was there and took her to the house; and Jessie went to bed, in a nice little room, and was asleep in a minute. Next morning, she opened her eyes and could not think, at first, where she was; then she heard the sweetest sounds, as if her canary had come too, and brought a number of friends with him. It was birds outside the window that she heard. She jumped up, and peeped out at the side of the blind. It was so lovely; instead of houses to look at, there were green fields with trees in them, outside the garden; and close by, under her window, was the garden full of bright flowers. The flowers and their green leaves were glancing in the sun, for they were covered with dew-drops, and so was the grass plot in the middle of the garden. She opened the window

to hear the birds better; and how sweet
the air was! She made haste to dress,
that she might go out. She spent a
happy week; and, when she went back,
her aunt let her pick a large nosegay,
to take to her papa and mamma.

Whit-Monday was come, and so Mr. and Mrs. Wood had written to their two sons, in London, that they hoped they would come down by the train and spend the holiday at home. Mr. Wood was a carpenter in a country village, and had a very pretty cottage. It stood in a green lane, with fields and trees all round; there was a pear-tree at one end, trained on the wall; the door had a porch covered with honey-suckle; in front was a little garden full of flowers.

Think what a pleasure it was for John and Thomas, who were working at trades in smoky London, to come there.

Jane and Martha, their two sisters, were busy getting ready for them all the week before. The parlour was cleaned, the windows made as bright as diamonds; the bedroom they were to have was scrubbed, and made fresh and sweet, for they were to stay all night, indeed they hoped two nights.

Then began the cooking: look what a large gooseberry pie Martha has made.

What a pleasure it was to meet at the station, and all come home together; and to sit in the evening in the porch, and tell all the news.

It was past Willy's bedtime, and his mamma had told him to go, but he would not go. " I do not want to go to bed ; I will not go to bed." This was the way he went on. Then he began to cry, and leaned against the door. His mamma was sitting out in the garden by moonlight: she was very sorry to see her little boy so naughty.

After waiting a good while she went in and shut the door. Willy was making such a noise that he did not hear her go: at last he looked up. He was alone in the garden. The moon shone bright, but he could not see his mamma near.

" Mamma, mamma!" he called out; "I will go to bed now." Then he went to the door and beat it; but no one came. At last he felt what a foolish boy he was! and how wrong he had been not to obey his mamma. " Come to me, mamma!" he began to say. He was crying, but with sorrow, not passion. He tapped gently at the door. Then his mamma opened it, and let him in. She did not speak to him, but led him up and put him into bed: she gave him a kiss; and he said, " Mamma, I am very sorry I was so naughty."

George, Emmy, Arthur, and little
Freddy played at soldiers. Jane had
helped to dress them up, and stayed to
look at them. George was the captain.
He had put on a paper cocked hat, and
had a sword by his side; in one hand

he held a gun, in the other a stick, to wave about.

Emmy was serjeant. She had a tall blue cap on, and carried a gun, and had red shoes to look as red as she could. Arthur was the drummer. He kept on drumming and making such a noise, that Emmy told him she could not hear the Captain's orders, and he must stop. Little Freddy was a common soldier. They had not a gun for him, so he was to pretend he had one, and to be sure to march about after the others.

They marched round and round the room. The drummer made a very great drumming and noise, and the captain and serjeant fired off their guns very often, always calling out "Bang!" when they had taken aim; and Freddy called "bang," too, though he had no gun. After a great deal of noise and shouting, the review was over; the drum beat very loud, and they marched round again, and that ended the game.

Almost all boys and girls have a
Christmas Tree now on Christmas Eve.
Here are a number enjoying themselves, and looking at all the bright
presents hanging on the tree. Would
you like to know their names?

The tall young lady, with a yellow frock and blue sash, is Rose; she is at home, and is giving the party. The little boy she holds by his hand is her cousin Charley. It is the first time he has ever been out at a party, for he is only five; and he never saw a Christmas tree before, and thinks it so very grand.

The boy and girl on Rose's left hand, are Frank and Lizzie; they live next door and have come to spend Christmas Eve with Rose. The boy in a blue jacket, red waistcoat, and white trousers, is named Fred; and that is his sister Jane behind him. They have just come in, and Rose is turning round to say, " How d'ye do, Fred?" in her pretty manner. More boys and girls will come soon. They will have tea and cake; then they will play games; and, after that, the presents will be taken off the Christmas tree, and something given to each. Then they will go home.

Mary expects her mamma home to-day, and runs out to the door, every now and then, to see if she can see her coming. Her mamma has been away in London for a whole week, and Mary wants her back very much indeed ; it seems so very long since she went. Mary has been in the garden to gather some fresh roses, and other pretty flowers, to put in water and place on her mamma's table, that the room may be sweet and bright when she comes ; and, before she goes in, she stops and listens in hopes of hearing her mamma's footstep on the walk. She has tried to make the garden look very nice too. She has picked off all the husks of the roses that had blown and shed their sweet leaves ; and she has picked any dead leaves off the other flowers, and pulled up any weeds she could see, and smoothed the borders with her little rake : and all the time her mamma was away, she has taken care of the plants in pots, and has watered them every day with her little watering-pot: and she has cleaned the canary's cage every morning, and fed him with his seed, and put fresh water for him in his bath and his drinking-glass.

Little Emmy and her mamma were going home one winter's day. It was only four o'clock, but it was growing dark in the London streets, and the Lamp-lighters were lighting the gas lamps. "Papa will be home first if we do not walk fast," said Emmy's mamma, So they walked fast. Emmy thought of nice home, of the bright fire in the dining-room, of going in after dinner and sitting on papa's knee and his telling her a story, and danced along, holding by her mamma's hand.

Just then, there was a sad sound near them. "O mammy, mammy!" They stopped, and saw, running by their side, a poor little ragged girl, crying, and Emmy's mamma said, "What makes you cry dear?" "I want mammy!" sobbed the poor child. "And where is she?" "At home, and I can't find the way. I am lost!"

Emmy was crying now. "O mamma!" she said, "how dreadful it must be to be lost! Let us take her home." So they

led her home, and gave her bread and
milk for supper, and nurse washed her,
and Emmy lent her a little night gown,
and she was put in a nice bed. Next
day they found out her home, and her
mother was so happy to see her again.

There was a Milkmaid, that lived at a farm house. She had to take care of six cows, and make butter and cheese. Her name was Dolly. It was summer, and the cows stayed out all night

There was Jetty, who was black and white; Spot, was brown and white; Brownie, was all brown. Then there were three small cows, mouse colour and white, that came from Guernsey, and their names were Maggie, Pet and Darling.

Dolly used to open the gate of the field, and set down her pails with a clang to make the cows hear. Then Pet was sure to stop eating and look at her. Pet was always the first to come to be milked. Her milk was so rich it was like cream, and there was one little pail called " Pet's pail," for her milk alone. Darling came next, and she had a pail of her own too. Then came Maggie. She was young and foolish, and would kick while she was being milked. One morning she kicked over

the pails and spilt all the milk. It was
very sad.

Jetty, Brownie, and Spot, wanted a
great deal of calling. There you see
Dolly with her pails going back to the
dairy.

"Welcome home, sailor boy! Where do you come from?"

"I have been a voyage to Bordeaux, in France, in the good ship LIVELY NANCY. We sailed from London, and steered down the river Thames; and we saw the North Foreland Lighthouse, and came into the Downs, and got into the British Channel. Then we steered to the southward, and at last we got to Bordeaux. We had brought flannels to keep the French people warm, and blankets for their beds, and broadcloth for their coats, and tweeds to make trousers for them. So, when we were clear, we loaded again with silks for the ladies in England, and wine for the gentlemen. Then we sailed homeward. I was glad to see the white cliffs of old England again. I climbed to the topmast this morning, at sunrise, to get the first sight of them. When we got off Sussex, the Captain says: 'Jack! what would you say if I put you ashore in the boat? You are nigh

your home here.' I jumped for joy,
and got my bundle. That's father's
cottage on the cliff. Hurrah! there's
mother coming to meet me, with Dick
and Polly. Good bye, little gentlemen
and ladies."

The poor man that you see making
the basket is quite blind. Blind people
can be taught to do many things; they
can make baskets, and mats, and
brushes, and several things. There are
schools where they are taught; and they

can learn to read, too. The books they use have letters that are raised, so that they can feel them; they feel about with their fingers, and find out by the shape what letter it is.

The girl you see at work, at a neat little basket, is the blind man's daughter. Her name is Sally; she helps him, if he wants help; and she makes the baskets that are smaller and prettier. Then, when they have made a good many, they bring out a little cart that they have, and their donkey that feeds on the common, and they load this cart with baskets and mats, and all they have made, and go about and sell them. Sally leads her father by the hand, because he cannot see to guide himself; and makes the donkey go the right way. Then, when they have been out all day, they count their money and see how much they have made. Sally puts away Eighteen-pence, to pay the rent, and they buy all they want with the rest.

Here is the Omnibus just starting
from a London street to some country
place; perhaps it is going to Hamp-
stead. At one of the windows a news-
boy is holding up a paper, calling out
its name; he wants some one to buy it.

" Only a penny," he calls out. No one seems to hear, or to intend to buy; but I daresay, before the omnibus starts, some one will put his hand in his waistcoat pocket, and find a penny and buy of the boy.

I wonder if the lady and gentleman coming along want to get into the omnibus. There is hardly room inside, I fear. The gentleman can go on the top, but what will the lady do ? Perhaps one of those gentlemen who are sitting there will give her his place, and go outside. I have often seen gentlemen do so. When it is fine it must be pleasant on the top, though a lady would not like to go there, and it would not be easy for her to climb up or get down, though a gentleman does not mind. But when it is raining, or very cold, it is best to be inside, and then it is very kind of a gentleman to give up his seat. Well, we should all try to be kind to each other.

This Organ-man has gone into the country; he has gone inside a gate, into a pretty garden, and is playing there, and some boys outside are standing to listen. Most likely there is a house in the garden.

I once knew a little girl who lived in the country, and who used to like to hear an organ very much. There was one organ-man that came every week to play to her; she called him "my organ-man." When she heard him coming up the lane, playing as he came, to tell her he was coming, she used to jump up from her play, or her work, or whatever she was doing, and run for her hat. Then she used to open the house door, and the garden door, and go out into the lane. It was very quiet there, with a pretty green field and trees, facing the garden gate on the other side. Then the organ-man used to stand under a tree and play, and she danced to the music. Round and round she went so prettily and merrily, holding up her arms in the joy of her heart. The organ-man looked so pleased to see her. When he had done, she ran in and got two-pence for him, and often gave him some milk and cake.

The holidays were come, and little Fanny, who lived at home, had had the joy of seeing her dear sister Lucy come from school, and had given her a pretty new doll that she had dressed herself. Lucy liked it very much, and named it Sylvia. Lucy had a great many stories to tell to Fanny about her schoolfellows, and the games they played, and the lessons they did; and Fanny had to tell Lucy about home, about the garden, and the ducks and the chickens, and all manner of things.

Aunt Jane was going to give a dance. Lucy was to go, but Fanny was too young; so she helped to dress Lucy, and Lucy promised to tell her all about it next day.

Lucy had a new frock to go in; it was blue, trimmed with red, and had pretty white lace in the sleeves. She had white shoes with red bows, and a red rose in her hair, and a red sash with a very large bow behind; in one hand she held a fan, and in the other

a bouquet of lovely flowers. Fanny
thought she looked very pretty. When
Lucy was gone, little Fanny went to
bed, and dreamed that she went to the
dance, and saw Lucy dancing and looking prettier than any one.

How very foolish it is of boys to be idle when they are sent to school! They are sent there for their own good. It does not matter to any one else half so much as to themselves, whether they learn anything or not; if they grow up poor dunces, that cannot read or write, the loss will be all their own. Other boys will be able to read nice books, and write letters to their friends, if they go away to some distant country, and read the letters their friends send to them; but the poor dunces can do none of these things. And now, only think how many young men go to other countries to get work, and get better wages, and get on better than if they had stayed at home; but how sad it must be for them if they cannot read or write! They can never get any news of the friends they have left at home, while those who can write, have sent letters home with money in them, to bring their dear fathers and mothers, brothers and sisters, out, and

been as happy together as they could
be. Now look at that foolish boy standing on a stool at the school-room door,
while all the others are at play; he will
not learn, so there he is with a dunce's
cap on.   Poor, foolish fellow!

Jack was a sailor boy, and had come home from sea after a voyage; and while he was at home, he was fond of roaming about with his little sister Polly. They lived near the sea; but what Jack liked best was to get into the woods, and there were very pretty woods near their father's cottage. Jack used to climb the trees; he got up to the top of the highest trees in no time. There he used to find squirrels' nests and birds' nests, and he would have taken them, only Polly would not let him. Polly went to school, and to Sunday-school; and the lady that came to teach them on Sundays had told the children how squirrels live in the trees, and collect a little store of acorns, and nuts, and fir-cones, for hard weather; and how little birds build nests with such skill, and rear their little ones; so Polly loved all these creatures, and could not bear to see anybody do them harm. She used to get Jack to sit down on the moss, at the foot of the

E 3

tree, when he came down, and tell him
stories about wild creatures that her
teacher had told to her.

Then they used to walk about hand
in hand, and she picked the pretty
flowers and told Jack their names.

Jane and her sister Emily had a party of their young friends to come to see them, and took them to see all the pretty places near. One day they made a plan to go to a hill where there was a fine view, and to have tea there. So their mamma ordered out the carriage. Under the coachman's seat was a hamper, packed with good things. But, when all had got ready, it was found that two were left without seats.

"I will tell you what we will do," said Jane. "Let John saddle the donkey, and lead him a little way, till we see that he will be good and go on, and Emily shall set off on him first. I will walk till I am tired, and then sit down by the roadside till she comes up. Then she shall walk and I will ride, and when I think she must be tired, I will tie the donkey to a hedge and walk on: then she will ride, and, by and bye, tie him again, and so we shall arrive in time." They went in this way; and, as the carriage got on long

before them, they found every thing
ready for tea on the hill when they got
there. The others had made a fire
with sticks, boiled the kettle on it,
spread the things on the grass, and it
was all very nice and pleasant.

One morning Charley went out to
play in the fields before breakfast. It
was very warm, and he felt thirsty.
There was a little girl sitting on a style,
so he asked her if she knew of any
water near. She said, no : but he could

buy milk from her mother. Charley pulled out a penny, and the little girl ran for the milk, and brought it in a mug. Charley thanked her, and asked what her name was. She said Molly.

"Well, Molly, suppose we play at something," said he. She said they could play at hunt frog, and began to run after a frog that was hopping among the grass; she soon caught it and squeezed it in her hand. "Put it down," said Charley; "you will hurt it," and he gave her arm such a slap that she dropped the poor frog; but she took up a great stone to throw at it.

"You nasty, cruel girl!" cried Charley, and he seized the stone and threw it at her. She began to cry. Charley was very sorry now. He led Molly home to his mamma, and she gave her breakfast and tried to teach her not to hurt creatures. She had taught Charley so; but she told him he was very wrong to throw the stone. That was not the way to teach Molly to be kind.

One cold morning in spring, as Bessy
was running about, she saw a little
brown thing that moved. She went
up to it, and what should it be but a
little robin that had fallen out of its
nest; so she took the poor little thing

between her hands, and carried it in to her mother. Her mother said she must keep it very warm, and try to feed it with some soft food, such as bread and milk, and chopped egg.

Bessy found some soft wool, and put it in a small basket, and made it hollow like a nest; and in this she placed the little bird, and then covered it lightly with more wool. Then she tried to make it eat, but could not. The poor little bird trembled, and shut its eyes, and looked very ill. "Oh dear, what shall I do!" cried Bessy. "It will die; I know it will die."

She saw a little bit of stick lying near, so she dipped it in the food, and took care to make a piece of egg go upon it; then she tapped at the beak, and, oh joy! the robin opened its beak and took the food. It got tame, and soon it could fly; but it came back to Bessy when she went out, and hopped in at the window, and sang to her, and was a great pleasure to her.

This poor boy is blind. He would
be very sad, if it were not for his kind
sister Amy; but she loves him dearly,
all the more dearly because he is blind,
and she leads him about, and reads
pretty stories to him, and plays with

him, and makes him as happy as she can. Poor fellow! He cannot see the green fields, and trees, and flowers, nor the bright sun, and stars, and moon, nor the faces of the friends who love him : but he has many pleasures. He can hear the birds sing, and the voices of those that talk to him; and smell the sweet scent of flowers, and feel the pleasant air and sunshine; and it is a great joy to him to hold Amy by the hand, and know that she is near him. He loves her very much.

He is to go to a school for the blind soon. There they will teach him to read. He cannot see the letters; but they make all the letters raised; then the blind people feel with the points of their fingers, and find out what letters they are. They will teach him also to make baskets, and mats, and many other things; and be sure Amy will always help him : and so, though he is blind, he will be able to earn a little and to be useful.

Did you ever hear any one play the
Guitar? This girl that you see in the
picture holds a guitar in her hands, and
is going to play on it. I think she will
sing too. She will make sweet sounds
come from her guitar, and will sing to

it. She does not look like an English girl. I think she comes from Spain. Her hair is dressed in a pretty way, and that black veil she has over her head, and hanging down her back, she can draw over her face if she likes. What a bright blue jacket she has on, and a pretty striped yellow and red skirt! Then look at the large bows in her shoes.

Some lady must have asked her to come in to her drawing-room, and play and sing; for you see she is standing in a fine room, and leaning against a table with a very fine red cloth on it. The lady will give her money for her music. Poor girl! I dare say she longs to go back to her own country, and will go as soon as she has made some more money. Her own country is much warmer than England, and has brighter blue skies; and, besides, all the friends she loves are there. It is sad to be far away from home. I hope she will soon be able to go back.

One day Kitty's mamma went out, and left her in the drawing-room, and said: "Be sure you do not go near the parrot's cage."

Kitty sat for a good while reading her story book, but then the parrot began to say, "Pretty Poll!" So Kitty got up, and began to go nearer and nearer.

"Poor Polly," thought Kitty, "she would like to come out; and, forgetting what her mamma had said, Kitty opened the cage door. Out came Polly, and flew to the arm chair, and perched on the back.

"Now Polly," said Kitty; "come back to your cage." But Polly never moved; so Kitty tried to catch her, but got such a bite from Polly's hard beak, that she screamed with pain. Polly screamed much louder, and made noises like laughing: "Ha! ha! ha! Oh, lau!"

Kitty sank down crying on the floor. When she looked up again Polly was gone; and, just then, her mamma came home. Oh, how sorry and

ashamed Kitty was! Polly had flown
out of the window; and it took
mamma, and Kitty, and all the ser-
vants, many hours to catch her; at last
they found her in a currant bush, and
she had stripped all the fruit off.

What is the matter with you, poor boy? What a woeful face you are making, and how you cling to your sister; I really believe you are frightened at the dancing bear. The other boys are looking at him and laughing. Do not be such a coward. I hardly know which makes most noise; that dog with his barking, or you with your crying.

You may be sure that the man with the drum and pandean pipes knows how to manage the bear; if he did not, he would not venture to bring him out among people.

Poor bear! I dare say he could cry, if bears ever did such a thing as cry, but I never heard of their doing it. I am sure he does not like being led about in this way, and made to dance; he is hot and tired, and feels very cross. I know he does. Look at his thick coat of hair; it was never meant for a country like this, and to go about among crowds of people in dusty roads and noisy fairs. He longs

to be far away, in his own cold country, in the cave in a wild forest, where he was born; it was a sad day for him when the hunters caught him, and brought him away to be tamed and taught to dance.

Blanche had a pretty little dog given to her; it was a Skye Terrier, with long hair, so long that its eyes were almost hidden under it. She named it Fido; it was to be her own little dog, that she was to take care of, and feed, and do every thing for. She used, every morning, to comb out his long hair, and then brush it with a nice soft brush, till it looked glossy. Then she gave him his breakfast, and then took him out for a walk. She was so afraid of losing him that she tied a piece of red ribbon to his collar and led him; but when he got older, and knew her better, she was able to let him run about alone without fear, if she was out with him: it would not have been safe to let him go by himself, because he was very pretty, and some one might have stolen him.

Fido had a basket of his own to sleep in, with clean straw in the bottom, and slept outside Blanche's door. When she was dressed in the

morning, and opened her door, out he
jumped, wagging his tail, bounding
round her, barking for joy, as if he
wanted to say how glad he was to see
her again; then she patted him, and
he was quite pleased.

Peter had his three cousins, Rose, Alice, and George, to spend New Year's Day with him. They played a great many games, he showed them all his toys and books. After dinner they thought they would dress up, and

Peter was to begin; he went out of the room, and, after a little while, in came such a figure! He had an immense face, a blue cap, a yellow coat, and a red cloak that trailed on the floor after him, and he went roaming round and round the room, saying: "Fee, Fo, Fum!" like the giants in Jack the Giant Killer.

At first they all burst out laughing; but, after a little while, Alice began to be afraid. "Do speak, Peter," she cried, "is it really you? Leave off saying 'Fee, Fo, Fum,' and say it is you:" but it was of no use. He went on marching about, and then ran after her and tried to catch her. She ran away, screaming, round the room, got on the sofa, jumped behind it, and tried to get out at the door. At last he drove her into a corner, and caught her, and she was almost crying, when George and Rose seized him behind, and pulled off his ugly mask and cap, and there was Peter with his good-natured face.

There was a fair at a village in Ireland, and a set of boys came before any one else, and got quite tired of waiting. There they stood by an old wall, and it was cold, and they began to feel cross, and were very hungry; so one of them, his name was Pat O'Grady, said he would dance a hornpipe. There you may see him dancing. He looked very gay, for he had put on his father's red waistcoat; it was too large for him, but he did not care for that, and he went on so merrily that the others began to laugh; at least Mike Tooley, that had a blue coat and yellow trousers, did; but Dan Crowter still looked cross.

While Pat was dancing, little Miss Gorman, the farmer's daughter, came by with her two little brothers, and stood looking at him and laughing. "Well done!" she cried, as he ended with a caper. "And it is well done," said Pat, "if you knew how hungry I am." Away she ran to her father, who was in the field. "Give them some breakfast, father," she said; "he does dance so nimbly"

So the farmer called them in, and gave them a good mess of potatoes and herrings; and Pat danced his hornpipe again to thank him.

This is a picture of a poor Slave Girl, of New Orleans, in the United States. She has got a task to do, and is working hard to do it; but see how she has started at the sound of some one coming: she is afraid she may not have done her work rightly, and that she will be beaten.

But there is joyful news in the world now. There are no more slaves in all that great country, the United States; they are all set free. Is not that joyful news? England had set her slaves free years ago; and now there will not, much longer, be any slaves in countries that call themselves Christian. In other countries, where people are savage and know no better, there still will be.

The poor black people that were slaves are very badly off, a great many of them. Some have not found masters; some are idle, now they are not driven to work with the whip; some are very stupid and helpless, for when they were slaves no one taught them any-thing. Many kind people are trying to teach them and help them.

Be joyful, little children, that you live in days when slavery is coming to an end.